P9-DTB-267
NO LONGER PROPERTY OF
SEATTLE PUBLIC LIBRARY

Miles of Smiles

by KAREN KAUFMAN ORLOFF illustrations by LUCIANO LOZANO

STERLING CHILDREN'S BOOKS
New York

Baby gives her mom a smile.
Mommy keeps it for a while.

She passes it to Mrs. Glass,
who shares it with her first-grade class.

The smile makes Sebastian beam.

He takes it to his soccer team.

The score is down. Coach starts to mope.

Roberto's smile
gives him hope.

It makes its way to Valerie,
who missed the goal and hurt her knee.

Val sends the smile to her Gran.

It goes to Jim, the garbage man.

Jim takes the smile to his boss,
who's had a day that made him cross.

His boss goes out for dinner later.
The smile cheers up Ed, the waiter.

Ed gives it to a boy named Shane,
to soothe him when he breaks his train.

When Shane arrives at Grandpa's place,
the smile brightens up his face.

Gramps walks the smile across the street,
and gives his neighbor, Anne, a treat.

Anne seals the smile in a letter . . .

. . . to make her sick niece, Jen, feel better.

Jen takes the smile for a run.
She waves to puppies having fun.

One pup who's made his getaway
sees Baby, and he wants to play.

The mommy laughs, then she thinks *maybe*—
Pup gives the smile back to Baby!

WELCOME TO OUR
NEIGHBORHOOD PARTY!!!!

Miles of Smiles!

To the "Soup Group"—Bobbie/Barb, Catherine, Della, Karen, Tracy, Val.
And thanks to my amazing editor, Meredith Mundy! —K. K. O.

To Baby Manso Prida. —L. L.

STERLING CHILDREN'S BOOKS
New York

An Imprint of Sterling Publishing
1166 Avenue of the Americas
New York, NY 10036

STERLING CHILDREN'S BOOKS and the distinctive Sterling Children's Books
logo are trademarks of Sterling Publishing Co., Inc.

Text © 2016 by Karen Kaufman Orloff
Illustrations © 2016 by Luciano Lozano

The artwork was created by hand, using mixed media, and then refined digitally.

All rights reserved. No part of this publication may be reproduced, stored in a retrieval system,
or transmitted in any form or by any means (including electronic, mechanical, photocopying, recording,
or otherwise) without prior written permission from the publisher.

ISBN 978-1-4549-1699-4

Distributed in Canada by Sterling Publishing
c/o Canadian Manda Group, 664 Annette Street
Toronto, Ontario, Canada M6S 2C8.
Distributed in the United Kingdom by GMC Distribution Services
Castle Place, 166 High Street, Lewes, East Sussex, England BN7 1XU
Distributed in Australia by Capricorn Link (Australia) Pty. Ltd.
P.O. Box 704, Windsor, NSW 2756, Australia

For information about custom editions, special sales, and premium and corporate purchases,
please contact Sterling Special Sales at 800-805-5489 or specialsales@sterlingpublishing.com.

Art direction & design by Merideth Harte

Manufactured in China
Lot #:
2 4 6 8 10 9 7 5 3 1
01/16

www.sterlingpublishing.com